CW01202390

Queen Rory, The Banished

A. Carys

A. Carys

The characters and events portrayed in this book are fictitious. Any similarity to real persons, living or dead, is coincidental and not intended by the author.

No part of this book may be reproduced, or stored in a retrieval system, or transmitted in any form or by any means, electronic, mechanical, photocopying, recording, or otherwise, without express written permission of the publisher.

Copyright © 2024 A. Carys

All rights reserved.

BOOKS IN THIS SERIES

A. Carys

DEDICATION

waves enthusiastically Lauren! We made it!

A. Carys

CHAPTER ONE

The gardens are my favourite part of the palace.

Roses, baby's breath, wallflowers, ferns, forget me nots, columbine and common mallow all decorate the wild grass borders of the palace gardens. The groundskeepers keep the grass and flowers nicely trimmed, but they're left a little wild since when we were little, my siblings and I loved to run through the gardens and play in the overgrowth.

The gardens are especially beautiful in the autumn months, so beautiful in fact that my grandmother and I meet for weekly picnics under the willow tree. I turn left at the grassy intersection and walk toward the willow tree. I gently swipe the branches to the side and step inside, letting the branches swing back into place behind me.

"Aurora, you're late," my grandmother scolds lightly.

My grandmother, Queen Carena, is one of the loveliest people I know. While she may come across as strict and proper when she's out in public, in private she lives like she's twenty two and runs circles around her advisors.

"I'm sorry. Alessia was on the warpath this morning and I really didn't want to bump into her," I explain.

Alessia is my stepmother. She's your stereotypical evil stepmother, and she's made it known to me and my siblings that she will never be our mother. She told us that she will never act like we are actually her children, and that crushed us when we were younger and didn't understand why she didn't want us as her children. This happened three years after our mother died of sickness, My twin siblings, Jowita and Calix were five and I was six, nearly seven when our father married Alessia. We thought he might wait a bit longer, or never remarry, but it seemed to me that Alessia had been working on marrying our father for quite some time. The death of our mother opened up a spot for her, so she worked tirelessly to get our father's attention. And it worked, she got what she wanted, and my father became blind to the world around him. In my opinion, he wasn't ready to remarry, he didn't mourn our mother enough and that has come back and turned him into a shell of his former self.

My grandmother tuts as I sit down next to her.

"That woman is always on the warpath, it just so happens that your father wanted to visit your mother's grave today. He came to me this morning with such a sorrowful outlook on life and I was concerned about him. I sent him to the doctor who recommended some time away from the palace."

I nod, wishing I could've seen my father this morning.

"Do not let this get you down, my child. Let's enjoy this picnic in her memory, there will be time for sadness tomorrow," she says as she offers me one of her finest porcelain plates.

We spent the afternoon laughing and snacking on triangle-cut sandwiches, fondant covered sponge squares, cupcake cases with cucumber and pepper slices, and a refreshing mint and lemon infused drink. We have a wonderful afternoon, and from the way my grandmother is laughing and joking, her next topic of conversation shocks me.

"Aurora, I want you to know something, something I haven't told anyone else yet," she says as she takes hold of my hand.

"What is it?"

"As you know I am not a young Queen anymore, and recently I haven't been feeling my best. The doctor checked me over and notified me that he believes I have what your mother had."

She stops talking, doesn't say anything else as I feel my world crack in half again. It first cracked when my mother died, and it's cracked again now that she's told me she might die the same way.

"When uh—when did you find out?" I ask, feeling all my emotions bubble inside of me. Tears sting my eyes, and a ball of panic has lodged itself in my throat.

"Four days ago. But I don't want you to worry about that or cry over my impending death. I have lived a long life; a happy life, and I have accepted what will come," she says calmly and squeezes my hand again.

"But you're going to die," I whisper as a tear escapes my eye.

"My child, I'm not as young as I once was, and we both know that everyone dies someday. I'll finally be reunited with my Rowan, so I won't be alone. Please do not cry over this, I beg you not to, future Queen."

My words get stuck in my throat at the mention of her being reunited with my grandfather. But those words quickly die, and others get stuck in my throat. *Future Queen.*

"Fu—future Queen? What do you mean? My father should—he should be the next in line."

She shakes her head, "I've been revising my Will and have named you my successor. I do not want your stepmother on the throne and your father is too detached from this world to rule like a true King. You are next in line to the throne, and you will make a fine Queen."

"I wo—" I go to object, but she shushes me.

"You *will* be a good Queen; the best Queen the Eight Isles could ask for. Promise me you'll make me proud."

I swallow thickly and nod. "I promise."

CHAPTER TWO

When my grandmother told me that she was dying, I hadn't expected the end to come so quickly.

I change out of my nightdress and head down for breakfast. When I arrive, none of my family is here. Not even Jowita, who has made it her mission to always be first for breakfast.

I walk out of the dining room and head straight for the doctor's office, where Healer Maribel always takes her breakfast.

I knock on the door but there isn't an answer. I push against the door, and it opens, and I find no one, again. As I make my way back toward the dining room, a mess of voices distract me.

I make a light sprint toward the front lobby of the palace. I skid to a stop at the sight of my cousins. All

9

of them.

"Subin?" I call out as I make my way over to the group.

"Rory," she exclaims. "We're so sorry to hear about our grandmother. We all rushed over as soon as we heard."

I cock my head at her. "What do you mean?"

"You don't know?"

"Know what?" A bad feeling runs along my skin, making the hairs on my arms and the back of my neck stand up on end.

"Our grandmother, she deteriorated overnight," my cousin Alex says. "Did no one come and get you?"

I shake my head. "No. I—I came down for breakfast and no one was there."

"Let's go to her room. That was part of our instruction for when we got here, to visit her immediately," says my oldest cousin Elle.

The Eight Isles are ruled by one family. My family. 363 years ago, when Queen Nyla ascended the throne to become the first Queen of the Eight Isles, she ruled over all of them. But she couldn't manage the workload by herself, so she assigned representatives from each Isle to take up the leadership role.

Nyla ended up having eight children, one for each of the Isles. On each of her children's 21st birthdays, she gifted them the throne of an Isle. From there, each of Nyla's children had children who took over the throne of their Isle. They all become princes and princesses in their own right, with their mother remaining as the overall Queen. It's a tradition that has continued up until now, but my father will be the first of Nyla's descendants not to have the throne passed to him, whereas his cousins have already passed the throne to their children, my cousins.

We reach my grandmother's room. I knock on the door and my sister opens the door.

"Alita was meant to come and grab you as soon as you woke. She doesn't have long left," she says as she welcomes us all into the room.

"Aurora? Aurora, my child, come to me," says my grandmother.

I move through the crowd of people surrounding her bed. My father, Alessia, Jowita, Calix, our cousins. Her advisors and the maids, Healer Maribel and her long life friend, Velan.

I take a seat on the bed next to her. She smiles at me as I take hold of her hand.

"How are you feeling?" I ask.

She's propped up with pillows and tucked up under her favourite pink and lace edged duvet. Before answering, she tries to move backwards into the cushions but fails.

"Don't move, just rest," Healer Maribel says.

"I'm not dead yet. If I want to move I will."

I shake my head at her. "Grandmother, why didn't you tell me you were this advanced?"

"I wanted to enjoy our picnic like normal. I didn't want you fussing over me like I was about to die on the spot."

I nod in understanding. Tears are burning my eyes as she squeezes my hand.

"I'm going to be alright. I'll finally be reunited with my Rowan, and we'll be watching over you from above."

"I don't want you to go," I admit tearfully, my throat getting thick.

"I know, but you'll make a fine Queen." She motions for me to come closer until she can whisper in my ear. "In my wardrobe, there is a box. It's full of journals, and they are yours now. They'll help you, my child."

I nod and lean back. "Thank you."

"Anything for you, Rory," she says weakly.

The family stands and waits, my hand stays firmly clasped in hers until she gives it one final squeeze.

CHAPTER THREE

My grandmother is dead.

The Queen of Xirie and the Eight Isles has passed. She died peacefully, surrounded by her family at half past ten this morning. Arrangements for her funeral will be announced in due course.

The gathered crowd of Xirie islanders, all of them standing below the palace balcony, gasped and cried out at the news, and as much as I wanted to join them, I had to remain unaffected. I had to hold a united front with the rest of my family. My cousins joined me on the balcony; my siblings joined me as well alongside Alessia and my father. After the announcement finished, my cousins headed back to their own Isles to let their people know what has happened.

The family and staff left in the palace all dress up

in black clothing, myself included. I picked out my prettiest black dress, pairing it with the matching corset and shawl. A maid, Alice, comes in and pins my hair back before she guides me to the dining room where everyone has gathered.

My grandmother requested that her Last Will and Testament, which is currently with her Lawyer and Chief Advisor, not be read until after her funeral.

"Did your grandmother leave specific instructions?" the head Royal Undertaker asks.

I take hold of her list of wishes. "She wanted a beachfront memorial service before her ashes are scattered underneath the willow tree in the palace gardens."

"Does the willow tree hold great significance for her? If so, we can have a plaque made and plant it next to the tree," the Undertaker suggests.

"The willow tree is where they scattered my father's ashes after he passed," says my father, looking up just long enough to politely address the Undertaker.

"Ah, yes. I believe my father dealt with your father's funeral arrangements. We are more than happy to leave the scattering to you all, and if you wish for a plaque we can have that arranged."

"Thank you, and yes, we'd appreciate a plaque," Jowita says.

We work on the arrangements for close to four hours. It's tiresome, and at times all I want to do is cry, but I try and hold myself together, no matter how much I feel like I'm falling apart on the inside.

The Undertakers leave just after 4pm, heading off to prepare for the funeral that'll happen in five days' time.

Dinner comes and goes in a blur and when everyone else retires, I head towards my grandmother's bedroom. I step inside and head for the wardrobe. I open the doors to the wardrobe and dig through the mess until I find the box marked *journals*. I pull the box out and blow off the dust from the top of the lid. I head over to her bed and settle down on top of the covers and encased by the many pillows she always kept on her bed.

I take the lid off the box and pull out the first one, mentally thanking her that she stacked them from oldest to newest. The first being dated back in Year

290, the year of her ascension to the throne, and the beginning of a 75 year long reign.

I don't keep track of the time as I read journal after journal, but by the time nightfall comes around, I'm too tired to head back to my own room. So, I settle down with another journal, prepared to read until I fall asleep.

CHAPTER FOUR

I spent the days before the funeral in my holed-up grandmother's room.

I've read every single journal that was in the box plus the extra ones I found tucked under a pile of my grandfather's old clothes. Those journals were written by my grandfather, with contributions from my grandmother every so often.

While my grandmother's journals told me about being Queen, how to be successful and how to get people to respect your command. My grandfather's journal detailed his journey through royalty as an outsider and his marriage to my grandmother. When he was alive, his voice was ever so gentle, he was so kind and soft and that comes through in the journal entries. Reading the entries that were dedicated to my grandmother are so full of love that I feel a little empty on the inside. This man loved my grandmother with so much passion and devotion and I can only hope that one day I find the same kind of love.

But today is the funeral and I'm back in my own room. Both boxes of journals have a new home under my bed, safe and sound from the likes of my stepmother. Alice, one of the maids, informed me that Alessia has been trying to get into my grandmother's room, but since I've been in there the last few days she hasn't been able to. I'm not the slightest bit surprised by Alessia's actions, but as just in case, I've had Alice place two guards outside of my grandmother's room.

"Knock knock," says Jowita as she pulls my bedroom door open wider.

"Hi."

"Alice said to let you know she can do your hair if you'd like," she says as she takes a seat next to me.

"I'd like that. Is everything ready?"

She nods. "Yep. Everything is in place for the procession as well. The Director has informed us that the only thing left to finalise is the walking order of the family."

I nod. "I take it father hasn't even glanced at the list I gave him?"

"He hasn't, and I don't think he's even left his room. He's regressing further into himself, Rory."

I sigh and nod. "I know, but there's nothing we can do. We tried everything and even grandmother tried to step in, but it didn't work."

"It's Alessia, isn't it? She's making him worse."

"She's not making him better, that's for sure. But just leave him be, at least for the moment. If you could you have someone check that he is getting ready, that would be great, but other than that, no one is to bother him unnecessarily."

She nods. "What do you want me to tell the Director about the walking order?"

"I'll sort it."

"See you downstairs?"

I nod. "See you down there."

⁎

It doesn't take me long to sort out the walking order.

The Royal Guard procession will go first, the final row of Royal Guards pulling the coffin behind them. I will go next, with Calix on my left and Jowita on my right. My father and Alessia next and then Velan and Healer Maribel. The cousins will walk behind them in order of the length of service to their throne. Behind them, the staff who worked closely with my grandmother such as her Advisors and her maids.

I walk through the halls of the palace, making a beeline for the front doors. When I reach the doors, two guards pull them open and I make my way down the grand, marble steps. Everyone has already gathered under the arch at the front of the palace, so I make my way over.

"Everything ready?" I ask Jowita.

"All ready. Just waiting for you."

The Royal Guards get into position first, making sure to line the coffin up with the flower line that has been painted on the compacted gravel of the streets of Xirie. The family gets into position next, and we wait for the three gun salute. Once the salute has happened, we begin walking. We walk along the courtyard and out of the gates that surround the palace. We then head down the hill and down through the Isle.

As we walk, citizens line the edges of the roads. They gather in droves and bow their heads as we pass. My grandmother was widely adored by the public, they loved her and at every jubilee celebration, they showed her just how much they valued her, so to have them all come out and pay their respects means everything to me, and I'm sure the rest of the family feels the same.

We continue down the slightly sloped trial until the sea comes into view. As we reach the sand, the guards pull the coffin over to the podium. Myself and the family take up our seats as the Director stands behind the lectern, ready to begin the memorial. Just before he starts speaking, I take a peek behind me.

Citizens have gathered behind us, keeping a respectful distance so that we, as a family, can mourn the loss semi privately.

The Director begins his speech, he prefaces the speech by saying that it was something my grandmother had written. As he reads it, he seems to speak with the same amount of passion I'm sure she wrote it with. As he reads, I look around at my family, and like my own eyes that are streaming with tears, theirs are too. Once he finishes speaking, he takes a moment to let everyone compose themselves before he moves to light the memorial candle. He steps back, murmurs something under his breath before inviting us up one by one to light our own candles.

"The final part of this memorial includes the walk back to the Undertaker parlour where we will cremate Her Majesty, as per her wishes."

Everyone gets back into position, the same walking order as on the way down here. The only difference this time is that the citizens who joined us on the beach follow us back up. It's a solemn walk, but it's made better by the gentle violin music drifting into the air from the citizen parade.

✳

After leaving the Royal Guard procession with the coffin at the parlour, myself and the rest of my family head back to the palace.

We don't sit down to eat the delicious smelling

buffet right away, instead we head right to the large balcony where over 20 lanterns have been balanced on the edge. Something we do in Xirie, and the rest of the Isles, is light beautifully patterned lanterns and release them into the sky when someone has died. Everyone takes a candle from the tray laid on the table and uses them to light the lanterns.

"Three, two, one," counts Velan.

We all release the lanterns on one. We watch as they float up and over the Isle. We only go inside once the lanterns have turned into tiny specs, like little stars in the night sky.

Everyone in the family, including the palace staff, sit down to eat the buffet. Everyone is sitting in such close quarters to each other as we all share stories and our favourite memories of my grandmother. We eat until we're full and we drink until four bottles of sparkling cherry juice have been polished off. Healer Maribel is the first to retire, closely followed by Velan, my father and Alessia. My cousins go next, all of them heading to their rooms to rest and pack up ready for their journeys home tomorrow evening. Calix and Jowita head off next, leaving me all alone.

I rest my head against the back of the sofa and release a large sigh. Something settles in my stomach, something that isn't related to the amount of food I've eaten this evening. It's heavy and it's dark, and as I look around the room, I begin to worry that something bad is heading this way.

CHAPTER FIVE

The next day, everyone gathers in the living room for the reading of the Will.

I'm tense as I take a seat in between Jowita and my cousin Alex.

"Why do you feel like a stone?" Alex asks and I shrug.

"I didn't sleep well. I think something is going to happen," I say to him.

"Are you suddenly capable of usings a Glance's magic?"

I roll my eyes. "Don't be silly. Glance magic is dying out anyway, it'd be a miracle if I suddenly revealed as one."

Jowita leans closer. "Don't say stuff like that around Alessia, she'll have you burnt at the stake."

"She'll burn me on the stake regardless after this reading."

"What do you mean?" asks Calix, who I hadn't noticed was standing behind me.

"You'll see in a few minutes," I say just as the room goes silent and Maribel stands in front of the fireplace.

"In my hand, I hold the final Will and Testament of Her Majesty, Queen Carena. She has asked me to read this to you one day after her funeral," Maribel says as she looks around the room.

"I have been tasked with this as a neutral party to the family. To begin with, I'll start with dividing the assets that Queen Carena has left to particular individuals."

Everyone nods and Healer Maribel takes a deep breath.

"The children of the Isles, Elle, Christina, Sydney, Subin, Alex, Lesley and Danil have been left a variety of objects and artefacts that Her Majesty has requested you take and display in your own homes. After we are done here, I will take you to them and have them packaged so that they can be safely transported back to your own Isles."

My cousins all murmur and nod their heads at Maribel.

"For Calix and Jowita, there are also boxes for you in the Queen's chambers."

"Thank you," they both murmur and for some reason, Jowita seems to relax back into the sofa a little.

"Now, for the part where things get complicated. Queen Carena, upon being notified she was going to die of illness, changed her Will to reflect the adjustments to the Line of Succession she made the day of her diagnosis. In my right hand, I now hold the new Line of Succession document that lists Princess Aurora as the next Royal to take up the throne."

Chaos ensues.

My father, still half in another world, is outraged at the decision. Alessia turns to me and starts to shout at me. She berates me and spews lies about me forcing my grandmother into making the changes. Velan is silent in his actions as he tries to placate my father while Subin, Danil and Lesley form a wall in front of me. They keep me out of Alessia's reach until she turns on Maribel.

"This is preposterous. Clearly she made Carena change the Succession and her Will. We all know how close the pair of them were, I wouldn't be surprised if she had Carena killed just to move the process along," she says, pointing at me as she throws her accusations.

"Actually," Maribel starts. "Carena came to me to diagnose her and that is what I did. It was as much a shock to myself as it was to all of you that she was going to die a lot sooner than anyone thought. I was present for both the changing of her Will and the Succession. Carena was completely in sound mind when the changes were made. For now though, we must look forward into the future and begin the planning for the coronation. Carena also wrote that we are to announce the next Monarch after the reading."

Everyone murmurs and most come and congratulate me. I feel extremely overwhelmed as nausea swims inside of me, and all I want to do is drink calming mint tea and take a few deep breaths. But I can't, not until the announcement has been made and we've finalised the splitting of the assets that my grandmother wanted to give away.

As everyone stands up and gets ready to accompany Maribel so that they can collect whatever has been left to them, my siblings congratulate me again. Once they've wandered off, Alessia shoulder checks me, hard. I try to ignore her, but I can feel her breath against my hair as she whispers in my ear.

"Watch your back, Princess."

CHAPTER SIX

In the early evening, we gather on the balcony at the front of the palace.

The palace staff worked tirelessly through the afternoon to try and rewire the rickety radio speaker system we had set up a few years ago. Technology isn't the best here, we're not very advanced, but the radio that was discovered in a cave many miles away has served us well.

Maribel stands next to me, adjusting the radio phone for me to speak into. Jowita, Calix and all of the cousins have joined me for this announcement as well. They've all been speaking very fondly of my impending reign, congratulating me and offering trade deals and other official connections I'll need to replace once I ascend the throne. It's been very overwhelming, and I have to resist the urge to tell them to shut up. A moment of peace and quiet would be greatly appreciated right now, and maybe even a little time to let myself properly digest the fact that my grandmother is dead. Despite seven days having passed, I don't think I've actually managed to wrap my head around it all. I don't think I've managed to grasp the fact that I will be Queen. *The Queen of the Eight Isles.*

I peek over my shoulder as a shiver runs down my spine. Alessia and my father are standing at the far corner of the balcony, both of them looking extremely pissed off. Velan is standing with them too, he's right next to Alessia, seemingly keeping her in her place.

"Ready?" asks Jowita, pulling me from my thoughts.

"I think so," I tell her as I take a deep breath.

Maribel taps the radio phone. The feedback makes everyone wince, but it also silences the crowd.

"Good evening and thank you for joining us. To start with, I want to introduce myself. I am Healer Maribel, the Royal family's personal doctor and executor of Her Majesty, Queen Carena's final Will and Testament. I would like to thank you all for the kindness and respect you have shown the Royal family in this time of mourning."

The crowd shuffles and places a hand over their heart before bowing their heads. A symbol of respect across the Isles.

"Upon reading the Will today, there have been changes made to the Line of Succession prior to the death of the Queen. Queen Carena's son, Prince Fabian was meant to ascend after either abdication or death, but Carena changed this order so that her eldest grandchild would become Queen. Princess Aurora, born to Prince Fabian and the late Princess Maria, will have her coronation next month, on what would have been the Queen's 76th year on the throne."

Maribel steps to the side and gestures for me to stand in front of the radio phone.

"Citizens of Xirie, it is an honour to be named as your next Queen. The death of my grandmother shocked both myself and my family deeply. I'm sure it did the same to you all as well. I miss her terribly and almost every night since she passed I have wished that she would come back to us, but I know that can't happen," I say passionately, pausing momentarily to collect myself. "So I swear to you all that I will do my best to be the best version of myself. To give my all to serve you until the end."

The crowd erupts into applause, and I feel a little better. Everyone seems so happy to have me as their Queen. Once the clapping stops, they all place their hands over their hearts and drop to one knee.

"Queen Aurora of Xirie," echoes through the air.

Both my siblings, Mirabel, my cousins and Velan all kneel as well, they cover their hearts and bow their heads. I scan over all of them and even find Alessia and my father doing the same, although it looks like they might be doing it begrudgingly.

Still facing my family, I cover my heart with one of my hands and bow my head back to them before turning round to face the crowd. I bow again, embracing my new title and the people who I will be responsible for.

CHAPTER SEVEN

Life gets busy.

Having just under four weeks to plan a coronation isn't a long time. So trying to get most of the difficult stuff done in the first week is proving challenging. Yesterday alone I had two dress fittings, approved both the Isle and palace decorations and went to a food tasting. As soon as I crawled into bed last night and placed my head down on my pillow, I was asleep. Having only woken up a few minutes ago, I'm still tucked up in bed and have no intention of leaving it until someone forces me to.

I seem to speak too soon as the door to my room bursts open and a frantic Jowita stumbles in.

"Rory, you need to come with me," she says as

she grabs my dressing gown.

"Why? What's happened?" I ask as I get out of the bed. I take my dressing gown from her outstretched hand and follow close behind her as she rushes back out of my bedroom.

"It's father."

"What do you mean?"

She stops to face me. "Guards flooded fathers' room this morning after hearing Alessia calling for help. He's dead."

My heart seems to forget how to work as it skips a few beats at the sudden news. "Dead? How?"

"No one is sure yet. Maribel is going to ask Constable Heidi to come and investigate."

"Investigate? Do they think someone had something to do with it?"

She shakes her head. "I've no idea. Maribel said we need to wait for the Constable to examine everything before she can tell us anything. Come on, everyone is in the dining room."

✳

It takes an hour of sitting in worry and sadness before Maribel and Constable Heidi have any news to tell us.

Alessia follows close behind them both, looking deathly pale and shaken. Despite my dislike for Alessia, I can't imagine what it must be like to wake up and find your husband dead.

"Thank you all for coming. I would like to start with my condolences for your loss, especially in such close quarters to the loss of Queen Carena,"

"Maribel, what happened to our father?" asks Calix. He's the most upset out of the three of us. He's been crying pretty much non-stop since he heard the news, and the only way to remotely calm him down was for both myself and Jowita to sit on either side of him, practically caging him inside of a drawn out hug.

"After performing an autopsy with Constable Heidi present, I can confirm that your father didn't die of natural causes. From the tests I ran, your father somehow ingested Silver Seed," she informs.

Silver Seed. Poison.

"How? Silver seed isn't kept or grown on Xirie," I ask.

"It does grow on Sacro Ridge though, an Isle that

37

has the most tourists travelling from there to here. It also isn't uncommon for the Black Market to transport Silver Seed between the Isles," Maribel states.

"So what happ–happens now?" Alessia asks tearfully.

"Constable Heidi will be launching an investigation into Prince Fabian's death and has asked me to assist her. Throughout today, you will all be questioned by the Constable so please be prepared to give accounts of your day yesterday and overnight. I also ask that you all hand over the keys to your bedrooms so that I can request a complete palace search in order to find out where the Silver Seed came from."

"Are we allowed to leave this room?" asks Velan.

"No, you need to remain here until everyone has been questioned and the palace search has been done," Heidi says.

Everyone nods in understanding.

Everyone nods solemnly. Things just seem to go from bad to worse. First my grandmother, now my father, and while in recent years my father and I haven't been as close, I still mourn a great deal for him. He tried his best, I know he did, he was just lost after losing my mother. He loved her so much, so deeply, that I don't think he quite knew how to move on with his life.

Maribel stands in front of me, bringing me out of my thoughts. I hand her the key to my bedroom, and she moves on. As I watch her collect the rest of the keys, the same bad feeling I had a few nights ago settles in my stomach again. It ebbs and travels through my body and thoughts of other things that could go wrong try to invade my mind. But what could possibly be any worse than my father dying?

CHAPTER EIGHT

One by one, everyone is interviewed by Constable Heidi and Maribel.

Velan goes first. Alessia goes second and comes back crying hysterically. A few of my father's personal guards are called into be questioned as well. Calix goes after them and now it's Jowita. She's been gone ten minutes and I know I'm next, and for some reason, I'm petrified.

The door to the dining room opens and Jowita walks in.

"How was it?" I ask her as she takes a seat on the sofa.

"Hard, but okay. Just answer the questions honestly and everything will be fine," she says, but something uneasy settles inside of me. The look in

Jowita's eyes is different to how it was when she was called. They're harder looking, the glistening from the tears has gone and it's like she is assessing me.

"Okay. Thanks," I say.

"Good luck."

I nod and get up. I walk to the dining room doors, push them open and slip out into the hall. I head straight to Maribel's office where she and Heidi are holding the interviews. A Royal Guard, who is standing outside of the office, opens the door for me. I step inside and the Guard closes the door behind me.

"Aurora, take a seat," says Maribel, her tone clipped. *Strange.*

"Thanks," I murmur.

"Can you walk me through exactly what you did yesterday?" Constable Heidi asks, and I nod.

"I got up at 8am. I took a walk around the grounds and then realised I was running late for my dress fitting at 8:45, so I skipped breakfast with everyone and headed straight to my appointment"

"Where was the fitting taking place and were you alone on your walk?"

"The fitting was happening in the lower levels of

the palace with Kyle and Cath. And yes, I was alone for my walk, but I walked past one of the gardeners."

Heidi nods and scribbles something down on the piece of paper in front of her.

"How long did the fitting go on for?"

"An hour, maybe an hour and half. They were doing the adjustments then and there so that they could start work on my second dress. After that I went to my first meeting to approve the decorations for the Isle and then I went back down to Kyle and Cath for the second dress fitting."

"What did you do next?"

"I went back up for another meeting about the palace decorations before heading to the kitchen where I spent most of the afternoon tasting different foods and cakes for the afterparty."

"Where did you go after this?"

"I went to the gardens."

"Alone?"

I nod. "Yes."

"And after the garden, did you go to dinner?"

I shake my head. "No. I went back to my room. I was tired so I decided to have an early night."

"And you didn't leave your room at all?"

"No. After I went to sleep, the next time I left my room was when Jowita came and woke me this morning."

Maribel nods. She doesn't say anything else and neither does Heidi as she finishes her note taking. When Heidi looks up from her papers and nods to Maribel, she turns to me.

"You can go and rejoin the others. We'll join you as soon as we get the results from the palace search."

I nod and get out of my chair.

"Thank you," I say as the door to the room opens, allowing me to leave.

I walk back to the dining room. The guards on either side of the doors pull them open for me. I step into the dining room and am greeted by my family who are staring at me. All of their eyes seem to track my every move.

"How was it?" Calix asks as I take a seat next to him.

"It was okay, nerve wracking though. How are you feeling?"

"It comes and goes. I can't believe he's dead."

43

"I can't believe it either," I say as I wrap him in a hug.

CHAPTER NINE

Waiting for the result of the palace search has left my nerves completely fried. I know that I have nothing to hide. I know exactly what I did yesterday and none of it included poisoning my father, but I can't seem to stop the worry that keeps snaking its way through my body. I know I'm not guilty, but for some reason the worry that I feel is linked to that. It probably doesn't help that everyone in this room keeps sneaking glances at me, almost like they are assessing me. Suspecting me? They all seem to share one coherent thought and that is setting me on edge.

Suddenly, Maribel enters the room, closely followed by Constable Heidi. Neither of them spare any of us a glance as they walk over and stand in front of the fireplace.

45

"After having the Guards do a full search of the palace, two vials of Silver Seed were found concealed in one of the bedrooms," Heidi announces as she holds up the vials.

Everyone gasps, including myself. Someone in the family or the staff did this to my father, on purpose.

"What bedroom?" I ask.

"Surprisingly, yours, Aurora."

Everything in my world freezes. Silver Seed poison was found in my bedroom. *My bedroom*. My cheeks burn with shock and tears burn at the corners of my eyes.

"My bedroom? Where abouts?"

"Hidden in your bedside table. Not a very good hiding place I must say, but a hiding place nonetheless."

"What happens now?" Jowita asks.

"It wasn't me," I blurt out.

The room begins to fill with Royal Guards, all of whom make a beeline for me. Calix moves away as I stand up, sizing up the Guards.

"Aurora, you are being arrested on suspicion of

the murder of your father. You do not have to say anything until the trial, but anything you do say could be used against you. Do you understand?" Maribel explains to me as two of the Guards grab my arms and cuff them behind my back.

"It wasn't me," I repeat as I look at my siblings, begging them with my eyes in the hopes that they'll defend me.

But they don't. Calix can't even look at me and Jowita slowly backs away, side stepping her way over to Alessia. *Traitor*. As much as the betrayal on their faces hurts me, I know I am innocent. I would've thought my own siblings would side with me and would defend me against these accusations. But they don't, and that is what hurts more than being arrested.

Before the Guards try to move me, I look at Alessia. While the tears have stopped pouring down her face, the fake watery eyes are still there and the slight smirk on her face tells me all I need to know. She's guilty. I could've told Heidi and Maribel that that was the case, but they wouldn't believe me, so I keep quiet. I don't say anything, I just let whatever is about to happen, happen without a fight.

I let the Guards escort me to the dungeons. I don't say anything when the Guards ungracefully, and with little care, shove me into a cell. I don't call out to the Guards when they leave and beg them to look again because I didn't do it.

I just sit in my cell.

Quietly.

Until someone in the cell next to mine starts talking.

"What you in for?"

"Murder. You?"

"Being a little mad. I'm Mayhem. Who are you?"

"Aurora, the now ex-Queen-to-be of Xirie."

"Shame, I had high hopes for you."

CHAPTER TEN

I stay in the cells for five days before I'm given a date for my trial. I then have to wait a further five days until they come and collect me.

During my time in the cells, Mayhem kept me company with his random wittering's and stories of what he got up to when he wasn't being kept in a cell. We talked about all sorts, mostly about what might happen to me if I'm found guilty, which I think will be the case. I've no idea what strings Alessia has been pulling, but I'm ninety nine percent sure that I'm going to prison for life.

"There's a safe space for you outside of these cells," he says randomly.

"What?"

"Up in the mountains you'll find a warm and

comfortable treehouse system where you can live peacefully."

"May, I'm in here for murder. I don't think I'll be making it out into the mountains any time soon."

"You will."

I shuffle on the wooden bed of my cell.

"You can't be serious."

"I've never been more serious about anything. Unfortunately, there are a few setbacks that will come before you make it there."

"What kind of setbacks?

"The kind that involves your death."

I choke on the breath I'm currently inhaling. "My what?"

"Your death?"

"Mayhem, please explain to me how I can live in a treehouse in the mountains if I'm dead."

"I can't tell you that."

"Helpful, thank you."

I hear him move in his cell, his manacled wrists clanging against the metal bars.

"Listen to me, Aurora, you are going to go through a lot in the next few days, but you will come out the other side. I swear to you," he says, and I can hear the conviction and promise in his voice.

I take a deep breath and try to swallow the lump that has formed in my throat.

"Thank you, Mayhem."

"Any time, Queenie."

I laugh at the nickname he's given me. I'm no Queen, not in the official sense anyway, but the time I've spent with Mayhem has made me forget a little about the situation I've found myself in.

On the day of my trial, I'm dragged by two Guards, still wearing my dressing gown from the day I was arrested, to the Court of Xirie where I had to appear before the Court of Citizens. The Court of Citizens wasn't called to assemble often, crime across all the Isles was low and a lot of the time, anyone found breaking the laws were given the minimum sentence that the justice system offered. One week in the village cells. It's not a lot, but it's enough to keep most people from reoffending.

The Court of Citizens assembles for a total of two hours before finding me guilty of the murder of Prince Fabian, my own father. Murder was the first charge, they then added conspiracy to overthrow the throne as the second charge. That charge is in relation to the changing of the Will and the Line of Succession. Somehow, the Court of Citizens were presented with evidence that I *made* my grandmother make the changes so that I would come out on top.

In my opinion, the second charge is preposterous, but there wasn't any room for argument, I wasn't there to defend myself and there was no legal aid coming to my rescue. It was just me and my alleged crimes. I know for a fact that Alessia had something to do with that second charge being added. I was the named successor in my grandmother's Will, and with the amount of people who seem to flock to Alessia's every command, it wouldn't surprise me if she managed to *persuade* someone to add it to my charges.

I tried to remain as unaffected as possible, knowing full well that Alessia was sitting in the audience. During my time on stand, where I was endlessly grilled about where I got the Silver Seed from, I took glances at my family. Calix and Jowita were there, sitting next to Alessia. They refused to look me in the eyes, only looking at the wall above my head or the floor in front of them. All of the cousins have turned up for the trial as well, but I struggle to be able to tell whether they also think I'm guilty.

"The Court of Citizens has decided that Queen Aurora of Xirie is to be banished to the sea. She will be walked along a pier before being left to the natural elements of the coastline. Whether she survives the waves or not, she will not be permitted to return to the centre of the Isle or cross any of the bridges to visit the sister Isles."

After the judge signs off on the banishment placed by the Council, I'm escorted to a carriage that immediately takes off towards the pier. I try to make conversation with the Royal Guard, but he ignores me the entire time. Thankfully though, he provides me with a change of clothes and leaves me to change in the privacy of the windowless carriage. Once changed, I knock on the door and the Guard helps me out of the carriage. He guides me along the shoreline until we reach the pier, at which point he all but drags me up the slope until our shoes hit the wooden slabs.

I look behind me as we reach the edge of the pier and see that a crowd has gathered. They watch as the Guard preps me, he gives me a hair tie so that I can tie it out of my face. He then asks me to take my shoes off. I do so and as I turn to give him my shoes, his arm suddenly shoots out and hits me square in the chest. I stumble backwards and I wave my arms to try to steady myself, but it's no use and I fall right off the edge of the pier.

I scream and then suddenly I'm submerged in cold water that shocks my body. I gasp and sputter as I resurface, and my arms violently flapping around. I continue to bob up and down, my head getting submerged repeatedly. I struggle to stay afloat and the more I fight the water, the weaker I feel myself becoming and the easier I find it to just let go.

I'm dead? I think I might be. Everything hurts and I feel weighed down by the water I was left to drown in.

"Ah, you're waking up," a feminine voice says.

I try to open my eyes, but the sun is too bright, and it burns my eyes.

"There's no rush, I'm not finished yet."

Those words take a second to register, and when they do, I practically jump up and scarper away.

"Who are you?"

"Queen Aurora, you're safe with me. I'm here to help."

She gets up from where she'd just been perched on the sand and comes over to me.

The sand.

Oh my god. The sand. I'm on the shoreline.

"Am I alive?"

"Yes. You survived the banishment to the sea, but only by a small amount. If I hadn't pulled you out when I did, you would've drowned."

"Where am I?"

"The old shorelines of Xirie, by the mountains."

"The mountains. Mayhem said the mountains were a safe place for me," I murmur to myself, remembering one of our conversations.

"Mayhem spoke to you then?"

"He did, we were in the cells together. He told me

of the treehouses in the mountains."

"I will take you to them, but for the moment, there is something I must do," she says as she crouches down in front of me.

"What—what are you going to—ahh."

My questions fall on deaf ears as the woman thrusts her hand forward and seemingly into my chest, and I do mean into. I grab at her arm and try to pull it back out, but she doesn't budge.

"T—take—take your hand out of m—me."

She nods and pulls her hand out, but it doesn't come out empty. She seems to bring my heart out with her.

"You've—my heart."

"It's not what it looks like, Your Highness, but I have a job that needs to be done."

"What job?"

"I must deliver your heart to the new Queen, to prove to her that you are dead."

"Ales—Alessia," I cough.

The woman nods.

"But I'm not dead. And why does she want my heart?"

"You're not, and that is a good thing. And the Queen wants evidence that you are dead and instead of asking for your body, she just wants your heart. But you are important to the future of Xirie, and I couldn't let anyone else get to you first."

"Important? Important how?"

"I cannot answer that. But I can tell you that the heart I took from you is a phantom heart, it is a replica of yours made of the same DNA in your own heart. It's a complicated spell and I had hoped to have finished it by the time you woke up."

"What are you going to do with it?"

"I'm going to deliver it to the Queen and let her know that you are dead. Before that though, I am going to take you to the mountains, to your new home."

I tilt my head at her, confused at what she means.

"I will explain everything to you in due course, but for now, let's get you to the mountains and start a fire, the last thing anyone needs is for you to die of a chill."

"I'm so confused," I admit as the woman helps me stand up.

"I know, but everything will become clear. I swear to you."

I nod and let this strange woman guide me to the mountains, to the treehouses that Mayhem told me about. She lights a fire and gives me a change of clothes before having me sit down. She gives me a metal cup of steaming water before she starts to explain everything to me, and I begin to understand the mess that Xirie has been left in since Alessia took the throne.

ABOUT THE AUTHOR

A. Carys is a self-published author from Portsmouth, United Kingdom. Other than spending 90% of her day writing, she also loves to crochet, read, and take photos of her family's cats.

Printed in Great Britain
by Amazon

42362073R00036